Bunjitsu Bunny
Jumps to the Moon

Bunjitsu Bunny Jumps to the Moon

Written and illustrated by
John Himmelman

SQUARE
FISH

Henry Holt and Company
New York

SQUARE
FISH

An imprint of Macmillan Publishing Group, LLC
175 Fifth Avenue, New York, NY 10010
mackids.com

Our books may be purchased in bulk for promotional, educational, or business use. Please
contact your local bookseller or the Macmillan Corporate and Premium Sales Department at
(800) 221-7945 ext. 5442 or by e-mail at MacmillanSpecialMarkets@macmillan.com.

Library of Congress Cataloging-in-Publication Data
Names: Himmelman, John, author illustrator.
Title: Bunjitsu Bunny jumps to the moon / John Himmelman.
Description: New York : Henry Holt and Company, 2016. |
Sequel to: Bunjitsu Bunny's best move. | Summary: Follows Isabel, the best
bunjitsu artist in her class, as she makes friends, faces her fears, and more.
Identifiers: LCCN 2015042696 (print) | LCCN 2016021396 (ebook) |
ISBN 978-1-250-12940-6 (paperback) | ISBN 978-1-250-10536-3 (ebook) |
Subjects: | CYAC: Martial arts—Fiction. | Rabbits—Fiction. | Animals—Fiction. |
BISAC: JUVENILE FICTION / Animals / Rabbits. | JUVENILE FICTION / Sports &
Recreation / Martial Arts. | JUVENILE FICTION / Humorous Stories.
Classification: LCC PZ7.H5686 Brj 2016 (print) | LCC PZ7.H5686 (ebook) | DDC [Fic]—dc23
LC record available at https://lccn.loc.gov/2015042696

Originally published in the United States by Henry Holt and Company
First Square Fish Edition: 2017
Square Fish logo designed by Filomena Tuosto

3 5 7 9 10 8 6 4 2

AR: 2.8 / LEXILE: 490L

For Sabum Nim Arthur Blair,
kamsahamnida.

Contents

Isabel

Isabel was the best bunjitsu artist in her school. She could kick higher than anyone. She could hit harder than anyone. She could throw her classmates farther than anyone.

Some were frightened of her. But Isabel never hurt another creature, unless she had to.

1

"Bunjitsu is not just about kicking, hitting, and throwing," she said. "It is about finding ways NOT to kick, hit, and throw."

They called her Bunjitsu Bunny.

The Floating Rabbit

"I have a new challenge for you," said Teacher to his bunjitsu students. He pointed to two hoops on the floor, one on either side of the room.

"Each of you has to take a turn standing in one circle."

"That's too easy," said Wendy.

"And," continued Teacher, "you must move across the room to the other circle without touching the floor."

"Rabbits can't float," said Ben.

"No, but we can jump," said Max.
He stepped inside the hoop and ran
in circles to build up speed. Then
he leapt in the air, toward the other
circle.

He didn't even come close.

"Me next," said Kyle. He picked up a long stick and entered the circle.

"WAHOOOOOO!" shouted Kyle, and he pole-vaulted toward the other circle.

He didn't even come close.

Ben took his turn. He sat in the circle. He sat and sat and sat.

"Well?" asked Betsy.

"I'm thinking," said Ben.

"You can think outside the circle," said Betsy. "Let us try."

Hmmm, thought Isabel. *Think outside the circle. . . .*

Soon it was her turn. Bunjitsu Bunny sat in the circle.

"Kyle and Betsy, will you please do me a favor?"

"Of course," they said.

"Will you carry me over to the other circle?"

Everyone laughed as Isabel was carried across the room. They set her down inside the other circle.

"Well done," said Teacher. "What did you learn?"

"Sometimes," said Isabel, "friends can help us do things we cannot do on our own."

Bunjitsu Bunny Freezes

Isabel got a big part in her school play.

"You will be a great princess," said Betsy. "You are good at everything!"

"Thank you," said Isabel. "I have never been a princess, though. I will have to practice a lot!"

"I am just a flower," said Betsy. "I don't have to practice anything."

"Flowers are better than princesses," said Isabel. "Flowers feed bees. Bees make honey, and honey is sweeter than any princess."

"I would still rather be a princess," said Betsy.

Isabel practiced her lines every day. Betsy joined her and practiced being a flower.

Isabel practiced her songs every night. Betsy practiced standing still.

Day and night, Isabel practiced. She could say her lines and sing her songs backward and forward. Day and night, Betsy practiced standing still. She was very good at it.

Soon it was the night of the play.
Everyone showed up in their costumes.

"Betsy, you are a beautiful flower,"
said Isabel.

"Isabel, you are a beautiful princess,"
said Betsy.

The curtain opened. A spotlight shone down on Isabel. She looked into the audience. Everyone was staring at her.

"Go ahead," whispered Betsy the Flower.

Isabel the Princess opened her mouth. Nothing came out. She was frozen in place.

"'The princess wishes to see the prince . . . ,'" whispered Betsy the Flower.

Isabel was still frozen in place. She
had never been so scared in her life!

"Curtain down," whispered Betsy
the Flower. Down came the curtain.

"What happened?" asked Betsy.

"I . . . I think you would be a better princess," said Isabel. "I would be a better flower."

"Are you sure?" asked Betsy.

"Very," said Isabel. "Let's switch."

Betsy was the best princess anyone had ever seen onstage. The audience cheered and clapped.

"You were a very good flower, too," she said to Isabel.

"Thank you." Isabel laughed. "It's easy to be a flower when you're too scared to move!"

Coyote

One morning, Isabel was hopping down the path. CRUNCH went something under her foot.

"You broke my cup!" growled Coyote.

"I am sorry," said Isabel. She reached into her pocket. "Please take my cup."

Coyote grabbed the cup. "It is too small," he said. "Find me another." He gave it back to her.

"I broke yours, so I will make things right."

Isabel hopped off. She returned
with a bigger cup.

"It is the wrong color," snarled
Coyote. "Find me another."

"I will try," said Isabel. She hopped
off and returned with a different
color cup.

"The handle is on the wrong side,"
barked Coyote. "Find me another."

Isabel spun the cup around. "Now
it is on the right side."

"I still don't like it," grumbled
Coyote. "Give me another cup!" He
dove at the rabbit.

Bunjitsu Bunny turned, and
Coyote slid across the ground. He
stood up and leapt at her. CRUNCH
came a sound from her pocket.

"I think you broke my cup," said Isabel. She flipped Coyote onto his back. "Now *you* have to find *me* another."

Coyote darted off. He returned with a cup.

"It is the wrong size," said Isabel.
"It is also the wrong color."

Coyote started to leave to find
her a new one.

"But I will take it anyway," said
Isabel. She took the cup. Then she
handed it back to Coyote. "Now
take this as a gift."

Coyote's face lit up in surprise.
"This cup is just what I wanted.
Thank you!" he said, and ran down
the trail.

Ben walked up to his friend.
"I saw what happened," he said.
"Why were you so nice to him?"

"It is easier to end a problem
than to keep it going forever,"
said Isabel.

Message in a Bottle

One day, Isabel found a bottle at the edge of the river. She picked it up to throw it away when she got home. Then she saw a piece of paper inside. It read, HELP ME! I'M TRAPPED!

Isabel looked at the island across the river. *Whoever needs help must be over there,* she thought.

She rolled a big log into the water and pushed herself across with a long stick.

Suddenly, the current grabbed
the log and carried her past the
island. Isabel jumped into the water.
She swam as hard as she could
against the waves. When she made
it to the shore, she was very tired.

"I cannot stop now," she said.

Isabel called out, "Hello?"

"Go away!" shouted a voice.

"I am here to rescue someone. Are you stuck?"

The weasel brothers came out of the bushes. "No. Now, get off our island."

"Not until I rescue who I came
to rescue," said Bunjitsu Bunny.

The weasels charged at the
rabbit. They were so fast! Isabel was
still tired from the swim. As soon
as she got one out of the way, the
others jumped in.

This is taking too long, she thought. "I am not tired," she said to herself. "I am not tired. I am not tired." Finally, she believed it!

"KERPOW!" One weasel went
flying.

"HEEYIP!" Another weasel went
flying.

"BUN-HO!" The last weasel
joined them.

Isabel searched the island. No one
needed to be rescued.

She swam back across the river
and read the note again: HELP ME! I'M
TRAPPED!

She looked inside the bottle.
Ladybug looked up at her. A big
smile spread across Isabel's face.

"Are you trapped in there?"
asked the bunny.

"YES!" said Ladybug. "Please tip the bottle over so I can crawl out!"

Isabel did, and out crawled Ladybug. "I thought you'd never come back," she said.

"I am sorry," said Isabel. "Sometimes we run around in circles when the answer is right under our nose!"

Follow the Frog

Bunjitsu Bunny and her friends were sitting by the pond. Out hopped Bullfrog.

"Do you want to play a game?" he asked.

"Maybe," said Max.

"Whoever can do everything I do will be the winner," said Bullfrog.

"We're in!" said the rabbits.

"Ready? Follow the leader. Hop across the lily pads," said the frog.

"We are rabbits," said Wendy. "We can hop."

Hop, hop, hop went the frog.

Hop, hop, hop went Isabel, Max, and Kyle.

SPLISH! went Wendy.

"Ready?" asked Bullfrog. "Follow
the leader. Sing 'JUG-A-RUM, JUG-
A-RUM' like I do!"

"JUG-A-RUM, JUG-A-RUM," sang
Isabel and Max.

"JIBBLY-JIBBLY," mumbled Kyle.

"Another one down," said
Bullfrog. "Ready? Follow the leader.
Hold your breath as long as I can."

Bullfrog held his breath. Max and Isabel held their breath.

"Pbbbtttt!" went Max when he couldn't hold it any longer.

"Bunjitsu Bunny is almost the winner!" said Bullfrog. He reached behind a log and pulled out a bowl. "Yummy, yummy worms," he said. "Follow the leader!" He dropped a worm into his mouth.

Isabel picked up a worm and
held it over her mouth. Then she
put it back in the bowl.

"Some contests," she said, "are
better to lose than win."

Karate Crab

It was a good day for a picnic at the beach. Isabel spread out a blanket and unpacked her lunch. She had made herself a big, fluffy carrot muffin. She was about to dig in when she felt a pinch.

"YEOOWW!" she screamed, and jumped into the air.

"This is Karate Crab's sand, so this is Karate Crab's lunch," said the crab.

"Then *Bunjitsu Bunny* will move to another place," said Isabel.

"Too late," said the crab. "My lunch now!" He grabbed the muffin and scuttled down the beach. Isabel chased him. Karate Crab went down a hole.

"Rabbits can dig," said Bunjitsu
Bunny.

"Crabs can pinch," said Karate
Crab. He pinched Isabel's nose.

"OW! Stop doing that!" she
shouted.

CLACK, CLACK, CLACK went the
crab's claws.

Isabel sat down. "You can't stay
there forever," she said. "I will wait."

Bunjitsu Bunny waited. And
waited. And waited.

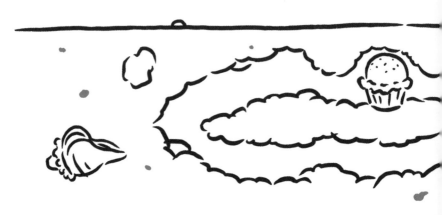

She was just starting to fall asleep
when she felt another pinch.

"YEOOWW!" she screamed, and
jumped into the air.

CLACK, CLACK, CLACK went the
crab's claws.

"That's it!" she said. Bunjitsu Bunny dug. Karate Crab pinched. Bunjitsu Bunny dug. Karate Crab pinched.

Dig. Pinch. "OW!"

Dig. Pinch. "OW!"

Isabel grew tired of digging. She
sat down on the sand.

"YUCK!" shouted the crab from
the hole. Out flew her muffin. "I
don't like carrots."

Isabel sighed. She was about to speak, but then she closed her mouth. Sometimes there is just nothing to say.

She walked back to her blanket and ate her muffin.

Oh, Thank You!

Jackrabbit was at it again. "I am the toughest rabbit in the meadow. I will fight Bunjitsu Bunny to prove it!"

"Jackrabbit wants to fight you again," Max said to Isabel.

"He always does," said Isabel.

Jackrabbit hopped up to them.

"Will you fight me?" he asked.

"No," said Isabel. "I don't want to."

"I will MAKE you want to," said Jackrabbit. He thought a moment, then smiled. "Bunjitsu Bunny . . . has short ears!" he said.

"Oh, thank you," said Isabel. And she walked away.

"I wasn't being nice!" shouted Jackrabbit.

He found Isabel later that day.
"Look at Bunjitsu Bunny's great big
feet," he said, laughing.

"Oh, thank you," said Isabel. And she walked away.

"I wasn't being nice!" shouted Jackrabbit.

Whenever Jackrabbit saw Isabel, he said something mean. Whenever Jackrabbit said something mean, Isabel said, "Oh, thank you."

"I WASN'T BEING NICE!" he'd shout.

One morning, Jackrabbit went
to say something to make Isabel
angry. When he opened his mouth,
something else came out.

"Bunjitsu Bunny is the nicest rabbit I've ever met," he said. Jackrabbit quickly covered his mouth.

"Oh, thank you," said Isabel.

"I didn't mean it! I didn't mean it!" he said.

Isabel patted his shoulder. "I have some bad news, Jackrabbit."

"Are you going to fight me?"

"No, I cannot," she said. "I think we are friends now."

Kicking Contest

"I have been practicing my kicks," Kyle said to Isabel. "I would like to try them out on Bunjitsu Bunny."

Isabel giggled. "Then *Bunjitsu Bunny* will accept your challenge."

"Just let me practice for another week, okay?" said Kyle.

"Yes. I will practice, too," said Isabel.

Kyle practiced every kick he knew.

Isabel practiced just one kick.

Soon it was the day of the contest.

"Have you seen how Kyle kicks?"
Betsy asked Isabel. "He is very good at
it!"

They found Kyle practicing in
the meadow. The other rabbits were
watching him.

"I call this my boulder breaker,"
he said. He kicked like a mighty bull!

WOOOOOOOOOOOOOOW

"Woooooooooooow," sang the
bunnies.

"This one is my mud slapper," he said.

"Woooooooooooooow," sang the bunnies.

"And this one is my thunder bopper. This one is my bomper romper. This one is my romper knocker. . . ."

On and on went Kyle.

"Wooooooooooooow," sang the bunnies. After the one hundredth kick, he stopped.

"Can we see what you practiced?"
Betsy asked Isabel.

Isabel stepped forward. "I practiced
this one," she said. She kicked into
the air.

"Just one?" asked Kyle. "I practiced
one hundred."

"Let's see how your kicks work," said Isabel. Kyle came at her with every one he knew. Bunjitsu Bunny simply stepped out of the way.

Kyle was slowing down. He tried to remember more kicks. A foot sent him flying.

Isabel bent over and helped her friend to his feet. "You did very well," she said.

"Thank you," said Kyle. "But you beat me with just one kick."

"Sometimes it is better to get *very* good at one thing," said Isabel, "than *pretty* good at everything."

Bat Cave

It was pouring rain. Isabel ducked into a cave.

"It is rude to sit on the floor in our home," said a voice from above. Isabel looked up. Three bats hung over her.

"How can I hang from the ceiling?" she asked.

"You are Bunjitsu Bunny," they said. "You can figure it out."

Isabel looked outside. It was raining very hard.

"It looks like I must." She sighed. Isabel leapt into the air and tried to grab the ceiling with her toes. She almost did it, but the rocks were too smooth. *That will not work,* she thought.

Isabel zipped across the floor, up the wall, and across the ceiling. When she got to the top, there was nothing to grab on to. She fell to the floor. *That will not work,* she thought. Then she had an idea.

Isabel gathered rocks from the cave and piled them almost to the ceiling. She climbed to the top and stood on her head. Her feet were pressed to the ceiling.

"Are you comfortable?" asked the bats.

"Not really," said the bunny.

The bats huddled together and whispered to one another. "Bunjitsu Bunny," they said, "you tried hard to be a good guest. We should try just as hard to be good hosts."

Bunjitsu Bunny climbed down to the floor. The bats joined her.

"Are you comfortable?" asked the bunny.

"Not really," said the bats. "But we are happy that you are."

The rain stopped. Isabel thanked the bats and left.

She returned a few days later to visit her new friends. This time, she was prepared to be a good guest.

"Are you comfortable?" asked the bats.

"Very," said the bunny.

A Promise Is a Promise

Teacher asked Isabel for a favor. "Will you watch my goldfish while I visit my mother?"

"I would be happy to," said Isabel.

He left his goldfish with her. Then Ben knocked on her door.

"I am going swimming," he said. "Would you like to come?"

Isabel REALLY wanted to go swimming! She looked toward the table.

"Blub . . . blub," went the goldfish.

"I can't go," she said to Ben. "A promise is a promise."

Wendy came by later in the day.
"My mom is making a clover cake.
Come over and have some with me."

Isabel REALLY liked clover cake!
She looked toward the table.

"Blub . . . blub," went the goldfish.
"I can't go," she said to Wendy. "A
promise is a promise."

A short time later, Kyle knocked on her door. "We are all playing bunjitsu tag. We need you!"

Isabel REALLY liked playing bunjitsu tag! She looked toward the table.

"Blub . . . blub," went the goldfish.

"I can't go," she said to Kyle. "A promise is a promise."

All of Isabel's friends were out having fun. She looked at the goldfish. "It is your fault I have to stay home," she said.

"Blub . . . blub," went the goldfish.

Teacher returned in the evening
to pick up his fish. "Why do you look
sad?" he asked Isabel.

She told him all the things she had
missed.

"Those are all your favorite things,"
said Teacher.

Isabel hung her head. "I should not be sad. A promise is a promise."

"I am very proud of my Bunjitsu Bunny. Anyone can keep an easy promise. It takes a very special bunny to keep a hard one."

Isabel smiled.

"Blub . . . blub," went the goldfish.

Somewhere
to Nowhere

Isabel went for a hike in the woods.
She wanted an adventure, so she
took a path she had never taken
before. After a while, the path split
in two. Owl dozed where the paths
separated.

"Excuse me, Owl," said Isabel. "Where does the path on the right take me?"

Owl opened her eyes. "Nowhere," she said.

"How can a path lead nowhere?" asked Isabel. "It has to go somewhere."

Owl had returned to her nap. Isabel took the path on the right. An hour later, she was back where she'd started. Owl still dozed where the paths separated.

"Excuse me again, Owl," said Isabel. "You were right. The path took me nowhere. Where does the path on the left take me?"

Owl opened her eyes. "Somewhere," she said.

"All paths go somewhere," said Isabel. Owl had fallen back asleep. Isabel took the path on the left. An hour later, she was back where she'd started. Owl still dozed where the paths separated.

"Excuse me once again, Owl,"
said the bunny. "I did travel
somewhere, but the path took me
nowhere."

Owl opened her eyes. "Where do
you want to go?"

Isabel thought a moment. "I want
to go somewhere that is not nowhere,"
she said.

"Well, that would be everywhere,"
said Owl. "There is only one way to
do that."

"How can I go everywhere?" asked Isabel.

Owl leaned forward and said, "Make your own paths."

Isabel smiled. She hopped off the path and headed for everywhere.

To the Moon!

Bunjitsu Bunny and her friends looked at the moon.

"I can almost touch it," said Ben.

"It seems so close," said Wendy.

"Can you jump to the moon?" they asked Isabel.

"Maybe," she said, "but I will need to practice."

Bunjitsu Bunny set out to practice every day. One week passed.

"Let's see how high you can jump now," said Kyle. Isabel ran right at him and leapt over his head.

"That is a very high jump!" said her friends.

"Not high enough," said Isabel. "I need more practice."

Another week passed.

"Can you reach the moon now?" asked Wendy.

Isabel leapt into the air. She sailed over a tall bush!

"WOW!" said her friends. "No one else can jump that high!"

"Not high enough," said Isabel. "I need more practice."

Another week
passed.

"You must be
able to reach the
moon now," said
Ben.

Isabel leapt
into the air.

"Where did she go?" asked Kyle.

"Up here," called Isabel from the top of a tree.

"How did you do that?" asked her friends.

"Not high enough," said Isabel. "I need more practice."

After a month had passed, her friends asked again. "Are you ready now?"

"Maybe," said Isabel.

They gathered under the moon. Isabel ran and leapt into the air.

She jumped very, very high but
landed on the ground.

"Not high enough," said Isabel.

"I need more practice."

A month later . . .

The Bunjitsu Code

All Bunjitsu students must do their best to follow the rules of Bunjitsu. If you wish to learn this art, you must read this and sign your name at the bottom.

I promise to:

- Practice my art until I am good at it. And then keep practicing.

- Never start a fight.

- Do all I can to avoid a fight.

- Help those who need me.

- Study the world.

- Learn from those who know more than I do.

- Share what I love.

- Find what makes me laugh, and laugh loudly. And often.

- Make someone smile every day.

- Keep my body strong and healthy.

- Try things that are hard for me to do.

GOFISH

QUESTIONS FOR THE AUTHOR

JOHN HIMMELMAN

What did you want to be when you grew up?
In order from kindergarten to high school: scientist, entomologist, veterinarian, cartoonist.

When did you realize you wanted to be a writer?
I always enjoyed writing stories and drawing pictures. I honestly cannot think back on a time when I didn't!

What's your favorite childhood memory?
Playing outside with my friends and brothers on summer evenings. There was no school the next morning, so we'd stay out past dark—under the streetlights along our little dead-end road. It was such an exciting new world. Maybe that's why I enjoy exploring and writing about the nature found at night.

As a young person, who did you look up to most?
Besides my parents, my uncle Roland. He was a soldier who came to live with us when he returned from the Vietnam War. I have two younger brothers, but he was like an older brother to me.

SQUARE FISH

What was your favorite thing about school?
Art class! It was always the highlight of my day. I was lucky to have very encouraging art teachers throughout my school years. And we got to listen to music during class.

What were your hobbies as a kid? What are your hobbies now?
I was really into bugs. I used to collect all different kinds and keep them in jars in my room. I'd study them for hours and hours, often drawing them. Now? I practice martial arts, play guitar, watch birds, chase butterflies, look for excuses to get together with friends, and . . . I collect all different kinds of bugs and keep them in jars in my room. I study them for hours and hours, often drawing them.

Did you play sports as a kid?
My dad would organize games for all the kids on our block. We played baseball, basketball, and football—depending on the season. I also played Little League baseball and CYO basketball.

What was your first job, and what was your "worst" job?
My first job was as a paperboy, delivering *Newsday* on my bicycle after school. It was also my worst job! I pedaled that overloaded bike through all kinds of weather every day of the week. Sundays were the worst! I had to get up at 5:00 a.m. to assemble the ad-bloated newspapers and then head out in two or three trips to deliver them. BUT, I made enough money to buy a new ten-speed bike and a camping tent!

What book is on your nightstand now?
There's never just one. *Shardik* by Richard Adams (I love fantasy—reading this a second time); *The Lost Civilizations of the Stone Age* by Richard Rudgley (I love history); and the *Handbook of Scottish Birds* by Peter Holden and Stuart Housden (getting ready for a trip!).

How did you celebrate publishing your first book?

I had just graduated from college (School of Visual Arts), having had my first book (*Talester the Lizard*) accepted by a publisher. I bought a 1980 Subaru Brat and drove cross-country from my then-home in New York to California. The celebrations of books to follow never matched that first one.

Where do you write your books?

I usually sit at a big desk in my studio, surrounded by snoring dogs and a chirping cat. Just to my right is a big window to my garden, meadow, and wooded yard. It could be said that I spend too much time staring out that window, but I'd disagree. Sometimes I give in to the call of the outdoors and move outside to write. Many of the Bunjitsu Bunny stories were written while sitting on a wooded shore by a big lake.

What sparked your imagination for the Bunjitsu Bunny series?

When I opened my martial arts school (with fellow author Ed Ricciuti), a local paper did a story on us. The reporter featured one of our talented Hapkido students, eight-year-old Isabel. I shared the article with Kate Farrell, my editor at Holt, who then urged me to write a story about a girl who is an exceptional martial artist. I made the girl a bunny, created the art of "bunjitsu," and a world was born. The thirteen tales in this book are gleaned from lessons I have learned in martial arts and in life.

All the names of the characters in the book are or were students in our school. The signatures on the Bunjitsu Code in the back are the actual handwriting of each of those students!

Do you know how to do martial arts?

I practice and teach Hapkido and Jeet Kune Do at my school, Green Hill Martial Arts, in Killingworth, Connecticut. We recently moved into a building built in 1881 that was once the town's meeting place for farmers, and then our old town hall. I love it there! I feel like we've become part of our town's long history!

What is your favorite thing about Isabel?
Isabel is very comfortable with who she is—so much so, she doesn't feel the need to prove her talents to others. But as skilled as she is, she's not perfect. She finds joy in conquering her challenges and learning new things.

What is more difficult for you: the writing process or the illustration process?
It depends on the book. The art for *Bunjitsu Bunny Jumps to the Moon* is done in a looser style than I've used in the past. It is sometimes hard for me to say to myself, "STOP! Put down your brush! The picture is finished!"

What challenges do you face in the writing process, and how do you overcome them?
In the thirty-something years I've been doing this, I still don't know if what I write will be of interest to others. I keep telling myself it shouldn't matter, but if you make a living as a writer/illustrator, it kinda does. . . . I still try to write for myself, though, and just hope that afterward there will be someone out there who will enjoy reading it.

What is your favorite word?
Betsy. It's attached to my wife.

If you could live in any fictional world, what would it be?
I don't think there's a fictional world that can match the one I'm living in now.

Who is your favorite fictional character?
Gandalf the Grey.

SQUARE FISH

What was your favorite book when you were a kid?
The King with Six Friends by Jay Williams, illustrated by Imero Gobbato.

If you could travel in time, where would you go and what would you do?
I sure would love to see some dinosaurs.

What's the best advice you have ever received about writing?
Fellow children's book author Kay Kudlinski always says, "Writers write!" So many people think about someday writing that story they always imagined they would write. Real writers don't think about it; they do it.

What advice do you wish someone had given you when you were younger?
"John, pay more attention in history class. You'll have less catching up to do when you realize there are no better stories than those of the people and events of our past."

Do you ever get writer's block? What do you do to get back on track?
I do. The best way to break through that wall is to write your way through it.

What do you want readers to remember about your books?
I want them to look at the faces in the pictures and know that as I was drawing every expression, I was wearing that same expression on my face. It's something I was told I do.

What would you do if you ever stopped writing?
I would find other ways to share stories, but writing is still the most comfortable way for me to do so.

If you were a superhero, what would your superpower be?
It comes down to the choice of being indestructible, invisible, or able to fly. Which would allow me the greatest advantage as a true force of good in this world? I tend to lean toward invisibility, but would not whine too loudly if either of the other two powers was bestowed upon me.

Do you have any strange or funny habits?
I sometimes pat my car and say "thank you" after getting home from a long trip. After years of doing this I found out that my grandfather used to do the same thing.

What do you consider to be your greatest accomplishment?
When asked this question, many people say their children. My son, Jeff, and daughter, Lizzie, however, are gifts, not accomplishments. So I'd say that finding a way to make a living that keeps me growing and learning, that satisfies my unrelenting need to create is a pretty big accomplishment.

Isabel is the best bunjitsu artist in her class. She can throw farther, kick higher, and hit harder than any*bunny* else. But can she go up against her toughest enemy yet—herself?

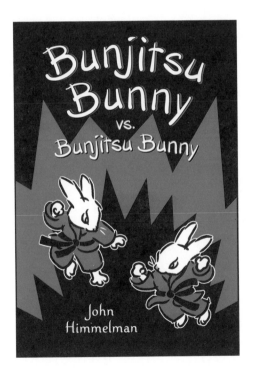

Keep reading for a sneak peek!

Shooting Star

Three bunnies sat looking up at the night sky. Isabel joined them.

"We are looking for a shooting star," said Max. "If you make a wish when you see one, it comes true."

A shooting star flashed overhead.

"I wish for a blueberry pie," said Ben.

"I wish for new bunchucks," said Wendy.

"I wish I didn't have to clean my room," said Max. "What do you wish for, Isabel?"

Isabel smiled and walked away.

The next morning, Ben found a big, warm blueberry pie waiting for him.

"My wish came true!" he said.

"I am so happy for you," said Isabel.

"Did your wish come true?" asked Ben.

"Not yet," said Isabel.

Later that day, Wendy found a
new pair of bunchucks next to her
old ones.

"My wish came true!" she screamed.

"I am so happy for you," said
Isabel.

"Did your wish come true?" asked
Wendy.

"Almost," said Isabel.

That evening, Max went into his room. It was cleaner than it had ever been.

"My wish came true!" he shouted.

"I am so happy for you," said Isabel.

"Did your wish come true?" asked Max.

"It did!" said Isabel, and she left the room.

Later that night, the four bunnies
met beneath the stars again.

"Our wishes came true," said Ben.
"But I think Isabel had something
to do with it. Did you bake me that
blueberry pie?"

Isabel blushed. "Yes," she said.

"Wait," said Wendy. "Did you make me those new bunchucks?"

"Yes," said Isabel.

"And I guess you cleaned my room," said Max.

"Yes," said Isabel.

"Will you tell us what your wish was?" asked Ben.

"I wished my friends' wishes would come true," she said.

"But you made them come true," said Wendy.

"It is easy to make wishes," said Isabel. "It is more fun to make them come true."

Follow along with Isabel
on all her adventures!

Read the whole series!